THE GREEK WHO STOLE CHRISTMAS

"Anthony Horowitz is the lion of children's literature." Michael Morpurgo

"Horowitz has become a writer who converts boys to reading."
The Times

"A first-class children's novelist."
TES

Other Diamond Brothers books
The Falcon's Malteser
Public Enemy Number Two
South by South East
The Blurred Man
The French Confection
I Know What You Did Last Wednesday

The Alex Rider™ books
Stormbreaker
Point Blanc
Skeleton Key
Eagle Strike
Scorpia
Ark Angel
Snakehead

The Power of Five™ series
Raven's Gate
Evil Star
Nightrise

Other books by the same author
The Devil and His Boy
Granny
Groosham Grange
Return to Groosham Grange
The Switch

THE GREEK WHO STOLE CHRISTMAS

ANTHONY HOROWITZ

WALKER
BOOKS

First published 2007 by Walker Books Ltd
87 Vauxhall Walk, London SE11 5HJ

2 4 6 8 10 9 7 5 3 1

Text © 2007 Stormbreaker Productions Ltd
Cover illustration © 2007 Martin Chatterton

This book has been typeset in Sabon

Printed in Great Britain by Cox & Wyman Ltd, Reading, Berkshire

British Library Cataloguing in Publication Data:
a catalogue record for this book is
available from the British Library

ISBN 978-1-4063-0485-5

www.walkerbooks.co.uk

CONTENTS

DEATH THREAT

I knew it was going to be a bad Christmas when I walked past the charity shop and the manager ran out and tried to offer me charity. It seemed that everyone in Camden Town knew I was broke. Even the turkeys were laughing at me. On the last day of term, the teachers had a whip-round for me ... not that I really needed a whip, but I suppose it's the thought that counts. Christmas was just a few weeks away and the only money I had was a ten-pound book token that my parents had sent me from Australia. I tried to swap it for hard cash at my local book-shop, but the manager – a thin-faced woman in her forties – was completely heartless.

"I need to eat," I explained.

"Then buy a cookery book."

"I can't afford the ingredients!"

"I'm sorry. You can only use a book token to buy books."

"What's the point of buying books if I'm too faint to read?"

She smiled sadly at me. "Have you tried Philip Pullman?"

"No. Do you think he'd lend me some money?"

I couldn't believe my parents had sent me a book token for Christmas, but then of course they had no idea about anything. My dad had moved them to Sydney a few years before – he was a door-to-door salesman, selling doors, and he must have been doing well because this year he'd printed his own Christmas card. HAVE AN A-DOOR-ABLE CHRISTMAS, it said on the cover. There was a picture of a kangaroo with a red hat on, looking out of an open door. I was still laughing as I ripped it to pieces. My parents had two new kids of their own now: Doreen and Dora. Two sisters I'd never met. That made me sad sometimes. They weren't even two years old and they probably had more spare cash than me.

I was thinking about Australia as I walked home from the bookshop. My mum and dad had wanted to take me with them when they emigrated, and maybe it had been a mistake to slip off the plane before it took off. While it was taxiing down the runway, I was running away to find a taxi – and they hadn't even noticed until they were thirty-five thousand feet above France. Apparently my mum had hysterics. And my dad had my lunch.

I'm still not sure it was a smart decision. They say that London is like a village, and I certainly enjoyed living there. The only trouble was, I'd moved in with the village idiot. I'm talking, of course, about my big brother, Herbert Timothy Simple. But that wasn't what he called himself. He called himself Tim Diamond, Private Detective – and that's what it said in the Yellow Pages, along with the line: "No problem too problematic." He'd written that himself.

Tim was the worst private detective in England. I mean … he'd just spent two weeks working in a big department store in the West End. He was supposed to be looking out for shoplifters but I don't think he'd kept his eye on the ball. In fact, the ball was the first thing that got stolen. After that, things went from bad to worse. The store had twenty-three departments when he started but only sixteen when he left. He was fired, of course. The dummies in the window probably had a higher IQ than Tim. He was lucky he had me. I solved the crimes, Tim got the credit. That was how it worked. If you've read my other stories, you'll know what I'm talking about. If you haven't, go out and buy the books. If you like, I'll even sell you a ten-quid book token. You can have it for nine quid.

Anyway, right now Tim was out of work. And November had arrived like a bad dog, snapping at everyone in the street and sending them hurrying home. As usual, it wasn't going to snow – but the pipes were frozen, the puddles had iced over and you could see people's breath in the air.

They were playing a Christmas carol on the radio as I let myself in. Tim was sitting at his desk wrapped in a blanket, trying to open a tin of sardines that was so far past its sell-by date he'd probably have more luck selling it as an antique.

I threw myself into a chair. "Any news?" I asked. "I don't suppose anyone has offered you a job?"

"I just don't get it," Tim replied. "You'd think someone, somewhere would need a private detective. Why is no one hiring me?"

"Maybe it's because you're no good," I said.

"You might be right," Tim nodded sadly.

"There are police dogs that have solved more crimes than you."

"Yes," Tim agreed, "but at least I don't have fleas."

I got up and turned the radio off. Tim had managed to get the tin open and the room was suddenly filled with the smell of twenty-seven-year-old sardines. And it was just then that there was a knock on the door.

I looked at Tim. Tim looked at me. We had

10

a client and we also had a room that looked like a rubbish tip and smelled like the River Thames during the Great Plague.

"One minute!" Tim shouted.

In that one minute, we raced around like two people in a speeded up commercial for Fairy Liquid. Papers went into drawers. Plates went into the kitchen. The sardines went into the bin and the bin went out the window. Sixty seconds later, the office looked more like an office and Tim was sitting behind his desk with a straightened tie and a crooked smile. I took one last look around and opened the door.

A man walked in. I guessed he was in his forties: short and fat, smoking a cigar. The cigar was short and fat too. He was dressed in a nasty suit. The pattern was so loud you could almost hear it coming. He had black, greasy hair, thick lips and eyes that would have been nicer if they'd matched. His shoes had been polished until you could see your face in them – though with his face I wouldn't have bothered. There was a gold signet ring on his finger. The way it squeezed the flesh, I doubted it would ever come off.

"You always keep your clients waiting outside?" he demanded as he came in and took a chair.

"We were filing," Tim explained.

He looked around. "I don't see no filing cabinets." He spoke like an American but he wasn't one. He was just someone who spent too much time on planes.

"We were filing our nails," I said.

He helped himself to one of Tim's business cards from the desk. "Are you Tim Diamond?"

"Yeah. That's me." Tim narrowed his eyes. He always does that when he's trying to look serious. Unfortunately it just makes him look short-sighted. "I'm a private eye."

"I know," the man growled. "That's why I'm here. My name is Jake Hammill and I want to hire you."

"You want to hire me?" Tim couldn't believe it. He leant forward. "So what can I do for you, Mr Camel?"

"Not Jay Camel. I'm Jake Hammill. You want me to spell it for you?"

"N-O," Tim said.

"I work in the music industry. As a matter of fact, I'm the manager of a woman who's a very famous pop singer."

Tim scowled. "If she's so famous, how come I've never heard of her?"

"I haven't told you her name yet."

"Maybe it would help if you did."

Hammill glanced at me. He was obviously suspicious. He turned back to Tim. "Can you keep a secret?" he asked.

"I'm not going to tell you," Tim replied.

"All right." Hammill nodded. "Her name is Minerva."

I have to admit, I was surprised. Hammill looked pretty small-time to me, but Minerva was one of the biggest names in the business. She was a multimillionaire pop singer and a movie actress. I doubted there was anyone in the world who hadn't seen her videos. She was the woman with the golden voice and the silver-plated breasts. Her clothes were outrageous – like the rest of her lifestyle. She had been born in Greece but now she lived most of the time in New York. The fact that she was visiting London had made the front page of every newspaper ... even the *Financial Times*.

"The thing is," Hammill said, "I've got a serious problem..." He twisted his signet ring nervously around his finger like he was trying to take it off. "Listen to me," he went on. "Minerva has been invited over here for Christmas. Tomorrow she's turning on the Christmas lights in Regent Street. And on Thursday at midday she's opening the Santa Claus grotto at Harrods department store in Knightsbridge. There's going to be a lot of press. A lot of TV. It's great publicity. But this is the problem..." He drew a breath. "I think she's in danger."

"What makes you think that?" I asked.

"Well, yesterday she received an anonymous letter."

"An anonymous letter!" Tim exclaimed. "Who from?"

Hammill scowled. "I don't know. It was anonymous. But it threatens her with death."

"So where is this letter, Mr Hubble?" Tim asked.

"It was sent to Minerva. She's got it. I'd like you to come and meet her at her hotel and she'll take you through it."

"She'll take me through the hotel?"

"No. She'll take you through the letter." He leant forward and already I could see the doubt in his face. "I have to say, Mr Diamond, I need to be sure you're the right man for this job. I wanted to go to the police, but Minerva's husband insisted that a private detective would be better. I understand you advertise in the Yellow Pages."

"Yeah," I muttered. "They match his teeth."

"I take it you know how to look after yourself," Hammill said.

Tim looked puzzled. "But I'm not ill!" he muttered.

Hammill rolled his eyes. Maybe I was imagining things but I could have sworn they went in opposite directions. "I'm not asking about your health," he said. "I need someone to stay close to Minerva while she's in London, and that may mean getting into a fight. So what I'm asking you is – do you know judo or karate?"

"Sure!" Tim nodded. "Judo, karate and

origami. When do you want me to start, Mr Rubble?"

It was obvious to me that Hammill was having second thoughts about Tim. And maybe third and fourth thoughts too. For a moment he bit his fingernail, deep in thought. Maybe he had plans to bite all the way down to the signet ring. Then he came to a decision. "All right," he said. "Minerva is staying at the Porchester hotel, which is in Hyde Park. That's highly confidential information by the way."

"What do you mean?" Tim demanded. "Everyone knows that the Porchester hotel is in Hyde Park."

"Sure. But nobody knows she's staying there. Otherwise we'd have fans all over the place."

"That would help with the ventilation…"

"Minerva likes her privacy. She's booked in under the name of Mrs Smith. Room sixteen. I want you to visit her this evening. Say, seven o'clock?"

"Seven o'clock," Tim said obediently.

"That's right. I'll let her take a look at you and if she thinks you're up to it, you're hired."

Tim nodded. I knew what was coming next. He was sitting back in his chair with his feet resting on his desk, trying to look every inch the private detective. The fact that he had a hole in one of his shoes didn't help. As far as he was concerned he was back in business.

15

And he was determined to prove it. "What about my fee?" he demanded.

"You're not hired yet," Hammill reminded him.

"OK, Mr Rabble. But I'd better let you know now, I'm not cheap. The only thing that goes cheap in this office is my budgerigar, and I don't think your superstar wants a body-guard with feathers."

Hammill tried to make sense of this, decided it wasn't worth trying and stood up. "I'll see you this evening," he said. One last twist of the ring. It wasn't going anywhere, but he was. He walked out of the office, slamming the door behind him.

There was a moment's silence.

I went over to the cupboard and searched through the CDs. I knew we'd have a Minerva recording somewhere and, sure enough, there it was – her third album, *Think Pink*. I looked at the face on the cover: the blonde hair, the green eyes, the lips that looked like they could suck in a horse. Not for the first time I wished we had a CD player, but Tim had pawned it months ago. Along with just about everything else. That was another sad thought. When I walked into the Camden Town pawn shop, I felt more at home than I did at home.

But maybe our luck was going to change. All Tim had to do was protect her for a couple of days and there'd be a handsome cheque at the end of it. He might even end up taking a bullet for her. If so, I just hoped they'd pay him extra. And whatever happened, it might be fun to hang out with one of the biggest entertainers on the planet.

"I can't believe it!" I said. "We're going to meet Minerva!"

"It's even better than that," Tim replied. "She's opening the grotto at Harrods. Maybe we'll meet Father Christmas!"

I slid the CD back into the cupboard.

Minerva had just received a death threat and her husband had hired Tim Diamond. That was like getting her a knitted cardigan when what she really needed was a bullet-proof vest. Well, one thing was certain: this was going to be a Christmas to remember. I just wondered if Minerva would still be around to see in the New Year.

SUITE SIXTEEN

The Porchester was in the middle of London's Park Lane, a five-star hotel that cost the earth. The sort of place I wouldn't be able to stay in a blue moon. You could tell it was expensive: I spotted two celebrities in the revolving doors and by the time I'd reached the reception desk I'd passed three more. There was enough fur and jewellery in that place to fill a store. And that was just the men.

The reception area was all glass and marble, including the receptionist's dress. That's fashion for you. Tim and I had arrived half an hour early to drink in the atmosphere – and looking at the prices in the hotel bar we certainly weren't going to be drinking anything else. A glass of water here cost the same as a glass of wine anywhere else, and for a glass of wine you needed to take out a loan. Nothing cost peanuts here ... not even the peanuts. That's the thing about the super-rich. They don't mind when things are crazily expensive. It just reminds them how rich they are.

We went over to the reception desk and asked to see "Mrs Smith". The receptionist was a slinky-looking girl with long fingernails. She had perfect teeth but she didn't smile and she spoke through her nose, so I guessed she didn't like showing them. She picked up a telephone and dialled a number with a fingernail that was a little longer than her finger. She spoke for a few seconds, then put the phone down. Her earrings jangled. So did my nerves.

"The second floor," she said, barely moving her lips. Maybe she was training to be a ventriloquist. "It's suite sixteen."

So Minerva had a suite, not a single room. We took the lift to the second floor and I have to admit I enjoyed the journey. It's the only lift I've ever seen with solid gold buttons and a chandelier. I could see Tim staring at everything as if he'd just died and gone to heaven. He'd insisted on putting on a suit, which he'd found at the bottom of the wardrobe. It was just a shame that the moths had found it first. Still, so long as nobody wondered why the jacket had seventeen buttonholes but only seven buttons, he'd be fine.

The lift door opened and we found ourselves in a corridor with about a mile of pink carpet, more chandeliers and the sort of wallpaper that seemed wasted on a wall. Suite sixteen was about halfway down – a double wooden door with gold numbers on.

Tim raised his hand, about to knock. And that was when we heard it. A sudden, loud crack from the other side. A gunshot? I wasn't so sure but Tim had no doubt at all. His eyes widened and he threw himself at the door – shoulder-first – obviously intending to smash it down, climb through the wreckage and rescue Minerva from whoever was taking pot shots at her. It didn't budge. Tim howled as he dislocated his shoulder. I reached out and opened the door. It was unlocked anyway.

We ran in. The door led straight into a plush living room. There were three people there. One of them was Jake Hammill, the manager who had come to our office that afternoon. The other was an older man dressed in a velvet jacket with a silk cravat around his neck. He had one of those permanent suntans that give your skin the colour of a peach but the texture of a prune. The third was Minerva. I recognized her at once with that strange buzz of excitement you get when you find yourself face to face with someone really famous. She was holding half a Christmas cracker. The tanned man was holding the other half. Well, that explained the bang we had just heard.

"Who the hell are you?" the older man asked.

"I'm Tim Diamond." Tim shrugged and I heard a loud click as his shoulder blade somehow managed to slip back into place. Well, that was something. Minerva looked as if she was about to call the police. At least she wouldn't have to ask for an ambulance too.

"So what do you mean just bursting in here?" the man continued. "Haven't you ever heard of knocking?"

"Wait a minute! Wait a minute!" Hammill interjected. "This is the private detective I was telling you about. The one you told me to see. Tim Diamond."

"What about the kid?" the man asked.

"I'm his little brother, Nick," I said.

"Yeah, well ... you'd better sit down."

Minerva had been watching all this with a mixture of puzzlement and disbelief. I sat down on the sofa next to her, thinking that a million kids would have given their right arm to be where I was right now and wondering what she'd do with a million right arms. She was dressed simply in expensive jeans and a white shirt, but even so she was one of the most beautiful women I'd ever seen. She had long, blonde hair, eyes that were somewhere between blue and green and the sort of body that made me wish I was older than fourteen. Maybe she was smaller than I'd imagined but then I don't have much imagination. And looking at her, I didn't need it. She was the real thing and she was right there next to me.

Meanwhile, Tim had sat down in a chair. I could tell he fancied Minerva too. As far as I know, Tim has never had a steady girlfriend. He just simply hasn't had any luck finding a woman who's attracted to a twenty-eight-year-old with no money and no brains. To be fair to Tim, he's not that unattractive. I mean, he's slim and he's dark and he's reasonably fit. And it seemed to me that Minerva was definitely interested in him. Mind you, if the old, wrinkled guy was her husband, I wasn't that surprised. How did a world-famous sex symbol end up married to her grandfather?

"So – how can I help you?" Tim asked with a lazy smile. He crossed one leg over the other and his foot caught a lamp, sending the shade flying.

"I told you," Hammill growled. "Minerva needs a bodyguard."

"With a body like that I'm not surprised!" Tim agreed.

"Hold on!" the old man interrupted. "That's my wife you're talking about."

"And who are you?" Tim asked.

"I'm her husband!" He was perched on the arm of the sofa next to Minerva. "My name is Harold Chase." He lay a hand on Minerva's shoulder, and maybe I was wrong but I could have sworn she shuddered slightly. "I'm paying you to make sure nobody hurts my baby."

"You've got a baby?" Tim demanded.

"I'm talking about Minerva!"

"I don't need looking after," Minerva said. They were the first words she had spoken, and I could hear the faint Greek accent fighting to get out. I was also reminded that this was the voice that had sold a billion CDs. "I don't need looking after"; it almost sounded like the title of one of her songs.

"We've got to take control of this situation," Hammill cut in. "You read what that letter said. Show it to Mr Diamond."

Minerva thought for a moment, then pulled a white envelope out of her pocket. She held it for a moment. "This arrived yesterday," she said. "It was slipped under the door of my suite. It's from somebody who hates me."

Tim opened the letter and read aloud:

"DEAR MINERVA, YOU ARE A MONSTER. I CANNOT FOREGIVE YOU FOR WHAT YOU DID IN TROPOJE LAST SUMMER. HOW COULD YOU DO THAT? I WILL NEVER FORGET IT AND VERY SOON I AM GOING TO KILL YOU. YOUR LIFE WILL COME TO AN END IN LONDON. THIS WILL BE YOUR LAST CHRISTMAS!"

23

Tim lowered the letter. "What makes you think that whoever wrote this hates you?" he asked.

Minerva stared at him. "I'm sorry?" she quavered.

"Well, he does call you *dear* Minerva…"

I snatched up the letter. It was straight out of a computer: blue ink on a plain sheet of paper. I noticed that whoever had written it couldn't spell "forgive". The envelope was addressed: Minerva, Suite 16.

"What happened in Tropojë?" I asked.

"Nothing happened in Tropojë," Harold replied.

"It's the concert," Hammill cut in. "It's gotta be!"

"Forget it, Jake."

"No, Harry. They might as well know." Hammill turned to us. "It was just one of those things," he explained. "It happened last summer, like the letter says. Minerva was going to give a big charity concert in Albania. It was to benefit OAK."

"What's OAK?"

"Overweight Albanian Kids. It tries to help kids who watch too much TV and eat too many McDonald's. Some of them have to wear elasticized clothing. Many of them are in wheelchairs. They can walk – they're just too lazy. Anyway, they were really looking forward to the concert, but at the last moment Minerva had to pull out."

"Why?" I asked.

"I had a headache," Minerva replied. Obviously the overweight kids of OAK had never given her much cause for concern. Until now.

"You upset a lot of fans, Minerva," Jake said.

"And you think one of the fans is out to get her?"

"That's what it looks like."

I wasn't so sure. The idea of an oversized Albanian TV addict travelling all the way to England to kill Minerva sounded a bit far-fetched to me. On the other hand, there was that spelling mistake: English clearly wasn't their first language. But there was something about the letter I didn't like – and I don't just mean the death threat. I knew there was something wrong. Something didn't add up. But I hadn't yet had time to work out what it was.

"My own feeling is that we should just get out of London," the husband said. "I can't sleep with the thought of you being in danger."

"Harold – you're exaggerating!" Minerva shook her head. "This trip is great publicity. Turning on the lights and opening the grotto is a big deal. I'm not going to run away just because some freak writes me a stupid letter." She turned to Tim. "I've got a single coming out on December twenty-fifth," she said.

"What's it called?" I asked.

Tim sighed. "It's called Christmas Day,

Nick," he said. "Everyone knows that."

"I mean – what's the single called?"

"It's a song about cowboys," Minerva said. "The title is 'Like a Virginian'." She fell silent for a moment and then she really surprised me. "If you boys are going to work with me, you might as well know that I hate this goddamn country and I hate Christmas."

"Minerva—" Harold began.

"Shut up, Harold! I just want to put my cards on the table."

"Your Christmas cards?" Tim asked.

"I don't have any. Those stupid pictures of angels and three wise men. If they were so wise, what was all that business with the gold, frankincense and myrrh? You think a baby's got any use for that sort of stuff?" She shook her head. "I hate everything about Christmas. Those stupid Christmas trees that drop needles all over the carpet. Those boring carols that go on and on. Santa Claus with his stupid beard."

"What about Christmas presents?" I asked.

"Why would I care about Christmas presents? I've got everything I want already." She realized she was still holding the half-cracker that she had pulled with her husband when we came in. "And I don't like these stupid crackers either," she went on. "They were sent up to the room by some fan or someone and all they've given me is a headache. As far as I'm concerned, the best thing to do with Christmas would be to forget the whole thing."

She threw down the cracker. A silver acorn and a slip of paper rolled out onto the table.

I don't know what it was that made me pick up the piece of paper. Maybe after Minerva's little speech I needed a laugh. Or maybe there was something about it that whispered to me that actually it didn't belong in a cracker. Anyway, I unfolded it and sure enough there was the same blue ink as the letter, the same typeface. There were just two lines.

```
    WHEN MINERVA SEES THE LIGHTS
THAT'S WHEN I'LL HAVE HER IN MY SIGHTS
```

I read it out.

"I don't get it," Tim said. "It's not very funny..."

"It's not a joke, Tim!" I exclaimed. "It's another death threat."

"But that's impossible!" Harold seized the piece of paper and held it with a shaking hand. "How did this get inside the cracker?" he demanded. He stared at Jake Hammill. "You brought them up here!" he continued accusingly. "What's going on?"

"I just picked them up from reception!" Hammill replied. "They said they'd been left in your name by a fan."

"What does it mean?" Minerva asked. Her voice had gone quiet.

Nobody spoke – so I did. "It must mean tomorrow," I said. "When you turn on the Christmas lights." I picked up the acorn. It was heavy – solid silver, maybe. "And look at this," I said.

"An acorn…" Tim was puzzled.

"Off an *oak* tree, Tim," I said. "They're telling you who it came from."

"Of course!" Harold Chase stood up. He was shaking so much, I was worried something was going to fall off. "That's it," he said. "We're not going to turn on the lights. Forget it. We're not going anywhere near them."

"Harold…" Hammill began.

"I mean it, Jake."

"Forget it, Harold!" Minerva had also got to her feet. "Look – I've already promised. I'm going to turn on these stupid lights. I've got to be there: the Mayor of London is coming. All the press will be out. It's going to be a big event."

"It'll be an even bigger event if someone shoots you," I muttered.

Tim turned to me. "That's a terrible thing to say, Nick!" He thought for a moment. "Anyway, they might not shoot her. They might run her over or blow her up or possibly fix the wires so she gets electrocuted…"

Minerva had gone a little pale. "Do you think you can protect me, Mr Diamond?" she asked.

28

Tim smiled. "I'm the private eye who never blinks," he replied. "And from this moment I'm not going to let you out of my sight. I'm going to walk with you, eat with you and go to bed with you—"

"Hey! Wait a minute! I'm in the bed!" Harold interrupted.

"We have a four-poster," Minerva said.

"That's great," Tim said. "We can have one post each."

Jake Hammill stepped forward. "I think Minerva will be safe enough while she's here at the Porchester hotel," he said. "Suppose Mr Diamond joins us tomorrow evening on the way to Regent Street?"

Minerva nodded. "I'm staying in all day tomorrow. That'll be fine."

"That just leaves the question of your fee, Mr Diamond," Hammill continued.

"No question about it," Tim said. "I want one."

"Of course." Hammill blinked uncertainly. "We'll pay you two hundred pounds a day. But let's get one thing straight. If anyone takes a shot at Minerva, we'll expect you to step in front of the bullet."

"Don't worry!" Tim jerked a thumb at me. "That's what he's for."

So there it was, signed and sealed. I still wondered why Minerva hadn't gone straight to the police – but maybe it wouldn't suit her being surrounded by the men in blue. I wanted to tell her that Tim would offer her about as much protection as a paper umbrella in the rain, but two hundred pounds was two hundred pounds. I watched as Jake Hammill counted out the money, and it occurred to me that the only time I'd been expecting to see the Queen that Christmas had been on her TV broadcast. But here were twenty little portraits sliding into Tim's outstretched hand. I almost wanted to kiss her. Or him.

We took the bus home. We could have afforded a cab but we'd already decided to blow a big chunk of the money on a three-course meal at our local Italian. I was already dreaming of a twelve-inch pizza on an eleven-inch plate. Extra cheese and pepperoni. And maybe extra pizza too. But even so, I couldn't get Minerva out of my mind. I went over what had happened in the suite. I was still certain something was wrong.

"If you ask me, Tim, there's something strange about this," I said.

Tim looked around him. "It's just a bus, Nick," he said.

"I'm not talking about the bus. I'm talking about Minerva. Those death threats! Whoever heard of a death threat inside a Christmas cracker?"

"Yeah," Tim nodded. "And there was no sign of a paper hat."

I shook my head. "I wouldn't be surprised if they weren't making the whole thing up ... the three of them. You heard what she said. All she wants to do is sell her CDs. Maybe the whole thing's just a publicity stunt."

Tim shook his head. "I don't think so, Nick. I think she's in real danger. Don't ask me why – I've just got an instinct for this sort of thing. A sixth sense."

"Sure," I muttered. "It's just a shame you missed out on the other five."

I looked out of the window. It had got dark a while ago and it looked as if it was going to snow. There were a few flakes dancing in the wind. As we turned a corner, I noticed a man standing on the pavement with a sandwich board. He was handing out leaflets about the end of the world. London is full of people like that. Maybe it's the city that drives them mad or maybe they're mad before they arrive and it's the city that attracts them. Anyway, this man had three words in red paint across his chest:

DEATH WILL COME

He seemed to catch my eye as we went past. And I found myself wondering. Was he just a harmless crank trying to sell religion to anyone who would listen?

Or did he know something I didn't?

REGENT STREET

Everyone makes a fuss about the Christmas lights on Regent Street and maybe there was a time when they were actually worth travelling in to see. I remember when I was small, my mum would take me into town and the lights would flicker and flash and sparkle and people would cross the road with their necks craned, staring at them in wonderment, and they wouldn't even complain when they were run over by the 139 bus.

But that was then. Nowadays the lights are more or less the same as they are on any other high street at Christmas. Worse than that, they're paid for by big business, so you don't just get Santa, stars or whatever. You get the latest characters from a Disney movie. Or "Harry Christmas" from J.K. Rowling. Or whatever.

Even so, turning on the lights is still a big

deal. If it isn't a member of the royal family, it's a pop star or a Hollywood actor. All the newspapers and TV stations record the moment when the button gets pressed, and the next day you can read all about it on page one: MINERVA LIGHTS UP LONDON. And just for one day the earthquakes and the wars and the dirty politics are left to page two.

We were driven to Regent Street in a stretch limo. The chauffeur was a tall, slim man in a grey uniform and I couldn't help wondering if someone hadn't stretched him too. Minerva and her husband sat on the back seat. For the first time I noticed he was wearing a hearing aid, but he didn't need it because no one was talking to him. She was gazing out of the window. It was made from special glass so that no one could look in. Her manager, Jake Hammill, had the next seat to himself. Tim and I were closest to the front – and furthest from the bar. The three of them were drinking champagne but all we'd been offered was a glass of iced water. Well, we were staff. Official security and its younger brother.

As usual Minerva was in a bad mood, but I had to admit that from where I was sitting she looked fabulous. She was wearing a bright red number with white fur trimmings. Think Father Christmas only thirty years younger and after major cosmetic surgery. Her lips were bright red too, shaped like a perfect kiss.

It would have been hard to believe that this was the woman who hated Christmas. She'd done herself up like the sort of present every man in London would want to open. I glanced at Tim and saw that he was drooling. I just hoped it wouldn't stain the carpet.

"Now, remember!" Harold Chase said to his wife. She turned round slowly and looked at him without a lot of interest. "You pose for the cameras. You make a little speech. You turn on the lights. And then we get the hell out of there."

"What's the big worry?" Minerva drawled.

"The big worry?" Harold's eyes bulged. For a nasty minute I thought they were going to fall out of his face. "There could be a killer out there, baby. You're going to be out in the open, exposed. Anyone could take a shot at you." He leant forward and turned to Tim. "You'd better keep your eyes open, Mr Diamond," he said.

"You don't have to worry, Mr Cheese," Tim assured him. "I've had my eyes on your wife all evening."

"Well, you'd just better make sure nothing goes wrong."

"What could possibly go wrong with me around?" Tim exclaimed. He threw his hands back in a gesture of surprise, emptying his glass of iced water over the driver.

The car drew to a halt. It was just coming

up to six o'clock on a cold, dry Tuesday evening, but the shops were still open and there were Christmas shoppers everywhere. We got out and suddenly the night seemed to explode in a thousand flashes. They came so thick and fast that I found myself blinded. It was as if I had entered an electrical storm that signalled the end of the world.

Of course, it was nothing so dramatic. Minerva was being photographed by a huge pack of press photographers, all of them holding up great, chunky cameras with lenses that were definitely pleased to see her. For a few seconds Minerva seemed to be frozen, half in the car and half out of it. Then she came to her senses and began to smile and wave; the silent, bad-tempered woman who had been sitting opposite me was instantly replaced by the perfect star that she was as the lights flashed all around her. And at that moment I got an idea of what it must be like to be a celebrity – loved not because of what you are but because of what the cameras want you to be.

At the same time, I was puzzled. Minerva had received two death threats. Even if she had decided not to take them seriously, her husband and manager had been worried enough to hire Tim and me. And yet here she was completely surrounded by photographers. It occurred to me that any one of them could have a gun. There were a few police around, but right now killing Minerva would be the easiest thing in the world. I said nothing. I could only stand there as she turned and smiled and smiled and turned while the photographers shouted at her from every side.

"Over here, Minerva!"

"Give us a smile, Minerva!"

"This way, Minerva!"

Tim nudged me. He was standing with his back to the car, blinking in the flashlights, but I could see that he was suddenly alert. I followed his eyes and saw a rather shabby-looking man in a suit hurrying towards us and suddenly I knew what was going to happen.

"Leave this to me..." Tim muttered.

"No, Tim!" I began.

But it was too late. Tim charged forward and grabbed hold of the man, then spun him around and threw him onto the bonnet of the limousine.

"That's far enough!" Tim exclaimed.

"I... I... I..." The man was too shocked to speak.

"What do you want with Minerva?" Tim demanded.

"I'm the Mayor of London!" the man exclaimed.

Tim looked suspicious. He was still pinning him down. "If you're the Mayor of London, where's your red cloak and pointy hat?"

"I'm not that sort of mayor," the man

growled. "I think you've been watching too many pantomimes."

"Oh no I haven't!" Tim replied.

By now, two policemen had appeared and had pulled Tim away, helping the Mayor to his feet. Because it *was* the Mayor, of course. I'd recognized him instantly – his bald head, his brightly coloured cheeks and his entirely colourless moustache. Jake Hammill had seen what had happened. He hurried over and placed himself between the Mayor and Tim.

"I'm so sorry!" he said. "We've hired private security and I guess he was a little jumpy."

"It's an outrage," the Mayor exclaimed. He had a whiny voice.

"Come and meet Minerva, Mr Mayor. She's been longing to say hello."

The thought of shaking Minerva's hand – or indeed any part of her – must have cheered the Mayor up because he seemed to have forgotten that he had just been attacked by Tim. Hammill took him over to his client, who was still posing for the cameras. "Minerva … this is the Mayor!" he said.

"How lovely to meet you, Mr Mayor!" Minerva sounded so genuine, I almost believed her myself. She kissed him on the cheek and night became day again as the photographers captured the moment for the morning's headlines. "Where do we go to turn on the lights?" she asked.

"This way..." The Mayor had gone red.

We made our way to a raised platform that had been constructed at the side of the road. There must have been four or five hundred people all around us, many of them waving autograph books and flashing cameras of their own. A Salvation Army band was playing carols. They finished "Away in a Manger" and began a version of "Silent Night" that was anything but.

Minerva climbed the stairs and I couldn't stop myself thinking of gallows and public hangings. I remembered the warning inside the cracker. Was someone really about to have a crack at her? I tried to think where I would hide myself if I were a sniper. I looked up at the rooftops. It was hard to see anything in the darkness but there didn't seem to be anyone there. How about an open window? All the windows in the street were closed. Then perhaps in the crowd...

By now Minerva had reached the top of the stairs. Was she being brave or stupid? Or was it just that she refused to take any of this seriously?

Jake Hammill was certainly looking nervous. So was Harold Chase. He was standing to one side, his hands in his pockets, pulling his black cashmere coat around him like he was trying to hide in it. His eyes were darting left and right. Even if nobody took a shot at his wife, I'd have said a major heart attack was a strong possibility. He didn't look like he'd last the night.

So there we all were on the platform: Minerva and the Mayor at the front, the rest of us grouped behind. There was a single red button, mounted on a wooden block, and a microphone. Minerva stepped forward. The crowd fell silent. The Salvation Army players came to the end of a verse and stopped – unfortunately not all at the same time.

"Ladies and gentlemen!" It was the Mayor speaking. His voice whined the full length of Regent Street and it wasn't just the fault of the microphone. "I'd like to welcome you all here and I hope you've all remembered to pay the congestion charge! We've had some great stars turn on the lights in Regent Street. But this year, if you ask me, we've got the biggest star of all. Please welcome ... Minerva!"

Everyone clapped and cheered.

"Thank you. Thank you so very much!" Minerva's voice echoed after the Mayor's. "I'm so thrilled to be here, at Christmas. It's such a wonderful time of the year – the birth of baby Jesus and of course my new CD is about to be released. So Happy Christmas to everyone, and here goes..."

She lifted her finger.

And that was when it happened.

There were two gunshots. They sounded

incredibly close and there could be no doubt that Minerva was the target. At once the entire atmosphere changed. There was a single second of frozen silence and then screams as the crowd panicked and began to scatter, people pushing each other to get out of the way. The band was swept away in the stampede. I saw someone fall into the big drum. The cymbal player was knocked off her feet with a final crash. On the platform, the Mayor had been the first to dive for cover. Minerva hadn't moved, as if unsure what to do. I couldn't see if she had been hit or not. With that bright red dress, it was hard to tell.

Then Tim leapt into action. I have to hand it to him – at least he was braver than the Mayor, who had curled into a ball in the corner of the platform with his head buried in his hands. Tim had been hired to protect Minerva and that was what he was going to do – even if the shots had already been fired. Even if she was already dead.

"Get down!" he shouted.

He lunged forward and I guessed that he meant to throw himself on top of Minerva – which, I had to admit, was quite an attractive idea. Unfortunately, Minerva had already stepped aside. Tim missed and landed, with his arms outstretched, on the red button.

At once, ten thousand light bulbs burst into multi-coloured life. This year the Regent Street lights had been sponsored by McDonald's. They depicted stars and Christmas trees decorated with twinkling hamburgers and fries. At the same time, a specially arranged Christmas carol – "We Wish You a McMerry Christmas" – boomed out of the speakers.

The Mayor opened one eye. "You idiot!" he screamed. "You've turned on the Christmas lights instead of Minerva!"

I'm not sure what would have happened next. Perhaps Tim would have ended up being murdered himself. But then Harold Chase stepped forward and pointed. "There!" he yelled. "There he is!"

He was pointing at the rooftops and now, with all the extra bulbs burning below, the darkness had become a sea of red and blue and yellow and white. And sure enough, high above one of the department stores, I could make out a short, plump figure half hidden behind a chimney stack. He was staring down at us and, although I couldn't see what it was from this distance, there was definitely something in his hand. A gun? He certainly would have had a clear shot at Minerva from where he was standing – but not any more. Half a dozen policemen had already reached the platform and they had all grabbed a piece of her. Jake and Harold were also grabbing at her. Tim had crawled off the red button and was trying to climb on top. The entire platform looked like a training session for the All Blacks with Minerva in the middle of the scrum.

The figure on the roof didn't seem to be moving and that was when I decided to take action. I didn't really know what I was doing. Part of me was asking questions. Why hadn't I seen the sniper earlier? Why hadn't he made a faster escape – or at least tried to fire off a few more shots? Was that a gun in his hand? And part of me knew that I wouldn't find the answers hanging around on Regent Street. I had to go and look for them myself.

I leapt down from the platform, pushed my way through what was left of the crowd and plunged into the nearest shop. It was a huge place selling clothes that I couldn't possibly afford and – one glance told me – that I wouldn't want to buy if I could. Blue blazers and red cravats have never been my style. There was a lift opposite the front door and I was lucky. The doors were just closing as I arrived. I ran in and pressed the top button – the sixth floor. I was lucky again. The lift didn't stop on the way up.

The sixth floor seemed to be devoted to Christmas presents for people you don't like: really nasty golfing jumpers, oversized umbrellas and multicoloured shoes. There weren't too many shoppers around as I burst out of the lift and made for the nearest fire door. Sure enough, a flight of concrete stairs

42

led up to the roof. I took them two at a time and it only occurred to me now that I was unarmed and about to come face to face with a would-be assassin who probably wouldn't be too pleased to see me. But it was too late to go back. And, I figured, he couldn't be more deadly than those golfing jumpers.

I reached a door marked FIRE EXIT and slammed into it … which, incidentally, set off all the fire alarms and the sprinkler system on the seven floors below. But now I was on the roof: a strange landscape of chimneys, satellite dishes, water tanks and air-conditioning units. I stopped for a moment and let my eyes get used to the darkness. Not that it was exactly pitch black. The Regent Street lights were still glittering below me and, looking down, I could see the scattered crowds, the police, what was left of the Salvation Army band.

Something moved. And there he was, the man that Harold Chase had seen from below. He was only about fifteen metres away from me, cowering on the other side of the roof. He didn't look like your typical assassin. He was short and very fat – almost spherical – with white, curly hair. I wondered if he was one of the overweight Albanians. It was Minerva's absence at a concert in Albania that had started all this.

The man looked at me with something between horror and dismay. He raised a hand as if to prevent me moving forward.

"No!" he shouted. "I d-d-didn't…"

Then he turned and ran.

I chased after him and that was when I discovered that I had miscalculated. I had run into the wrong store and there was a three-metre gap between his roof and mine. But I hadn't come this far to let an impossible jump and a probable fall to my death seven floors below worry me. I picked up speed and threw myself off the edge.

For a moment I hung in the air and I could feel the ground a very long way beneath me. The cold night air was rushing into me and – for a nasty moment – so was the pavement. The other roof was too far away. I wasn't going to make it. Suddenly I was angry with myself. Who did I think I was? Spider-Man? If so, I'd forgotten to pack a web.

But I didn't fall. Somehow my outstretched hands caught hold of the edge of the other roof and I winced as my stomach and shoulders slammed into the brickwork. I could taste blood and dust in my mouth. I'd cut my lip and maybe loosened a couple of my teeth. Using what little strength I had left, I managed to pull myself up and roll to safety. Painfully, I got to my feet. I wasn't surprised to see that the little fat man had gone.

He had left something behind. I saw them – three small silver objects on the asphalt. At first I thought they were bullets, but as I walked towards them, I realized they were too big. People down in the street were pointing up at me and shouting as I dropped to one knee and scooped them into my hand.

Three oak leaves. That was what the sniper had left behind. The acorn in the cracker and now this. He was definitely trying to tell me something and I'd got the message loud and clear.

DINNER FOR TWO

When I woke up the next morning, we were right back where we'd started. Which is to say, we were in Camden Town, in the office, and once again Tim was out of work. It turned out that nobody had been particularly impressed by my death-defying leap when all I'd got to show for it was grazed arms, bruises and a handful of silver oak leaves. I'd given the police a description of the man I'd seen on the roof – not that it added up to much. Small and fat. The curly hair could have been a wig. And although he had spoken, he hadn't said enough for me to be sure whether he had an Albanian accent or not.

As I'd sat in the bath that night, I'd gone over his words a dozen times. *No! I d-d-didn't...* Had he been scared or did he always stammer like that? And what had he meant? The police had decided that he was angry –

that he was telling me he hadn't shot Minerva in the sense that he had missed. To me it seemed simpler than that. "I didn't do it. It wasn't me." That was what he had been trying to say. But then why had he left the oak leaves behind? Maybe they were the symbol of the society for Overweight Albanian Kids. And finally, where was the gun? I thought I'd seen something in his hand but he hadn't had it when I reached the roof.

Anyway, the case was over as far as we were concerned. Now that the police knew Minerva was in real danger, they had taken over protection duties – and looking at some of those officers leering at her on Regent Street, I could see that plenty of them were going to be putting in for overtime. The good news was that we still had about seventy pounds of the two hundred Jake Hammill had given us. That would buy us a Christmas turkey, Brussels sprouts, roast potatoes and chestnut stuffing. It was just a shame that Tim had sold the oven.

I found him at breakfast with a bowl of cornflakes and the morning newspaper. He wasn't looking too pleased and I soon saw why. He'd made the front page. There was a picture of him spread out on his stomach just after he had accidentally turned on the Christmas lights.

"Have you seen this?" he wailed as I sat down. "And look at this!"

He tapped the caption underneath the picture:

DIM DIAMOND ASSAULTS MAYOR AND TURNS ON THE LIGHTS

"It must be a misprint," he said.

"Are you sure?" I asked.

Tim sighed – and suddenly he was looking sad. "You know, Nick," he began. "Recently, I've been thinking."

"Did it hurt?" I muttered.

He ignored me. "Maybe I should think about getting another job. I mean, look at me! I'm twenty-eight. I never have any money. I'm six months behind on the rent. I can't remember the last time you and I had a square meal."

"We had pizza the night before last," I reminded him.

"That was circular. And whenever I do get a job – like this business with Miranda – it always seems to go wrong." He sighed again. "She told me I was the most stupid person she'd ever met."

"Maybe she was joking."

"She spat at me and tried to strangle me!"

"Well ... she's Greek."

Tim shook his head. "As soon as the New Year begins, I'm going to find myself a proper job," he said. "It shouldn't be too difficult. I've got qualifications."

I fell silent. I didn't have the heart to remind

him that he only had two A levels – and one of them was in embroidery.

It looked as if we were going to have a pretty glum Christmas. But as you'll probably know by now, nothing in our lives ever turns out quite how we expect. A second later there was a knock at the door and before either of us could react, Minerva walked in. I was so surprised, I almost fell off my chair. Tim was so surprised he actually did fall off his.

She was on her own and she was trying to look inconspicuous dressed in jeans and a black jersey with a one-thousand-dollar pair of sunglasses hiding her eyes. But Minerva was Minerva. She couldn't look inconspicuous if she covered herself in mud and sat in a swamp.

"Minerva!" Tim gasped as he picked himself up.

"I didn't want to see you," Minerva said, taking off her sunglasses so she could see him better. "I didn't want to come here," she went on. "But I had to. Last night I behaved like a cow."

"You ate grass?" Tim asked.

"No. I behaved disgracefully towards you. I spat at you. I tried to strangle you. But this morning, when I woke up, I realized I'd got it all wrong." She sat down. "Harold brought in the newspapers and I saw that we got every single front page. And part of that was thanks to you. *The Times* called you a maniac. The

Mail said you were idiotic. The *Guardian* thought you were a banker."

"That *was* a misprint," I said.

Minerva ignored me. "If I'd just turned on those ridiculous lights, the most I would have got would have been the front page of the evening paper. But the way things turned out, I got more publicity than I could have dreamed of. Harold is certain my new CD is going to go straight to number one."

"How is Harold?" I asked.

"He had a very lucky escape last night," Minerva said. "One of those bullets missed him by a centimetre. It even burnt a hole in the side of his coat."

"You mean … it could have hit his pace-maker?" I exclaimed.

"It was a near miss. But I'm not here to talk about Harold." She turned to Tim. "I want to make it up to you, Timothy," she said. "I want to invite you to dinner. I've already reserved a table for two."

"Isn't two a little early for dinner?" Tim asked.

"For just the two of us, I mean!" Minerva smiled but I wasn't entirely convinced. I'd met sharks with friendlier teeth. "At eight o'clock this evening," she went on. "There's a restaurant I go to. It's called The Gravy." She giggled mischievously. "I thought we might have a little tête-à-tête."

"I'm not that crazy about French food," Tim muttered.

"You'll like this," Minerva simpered. "Make sure you dress up smart. You should put on that suit of yours with seven buttons and seventeen buttonholes."

And with that she was gone.

I went over to the window and looked out as she left the building. There was a police car waiting for her. It was true, then. The men in blue had now taken over Tim's job.

"They're giving her round-the-clock protection," I said.

"They think someone's going to kill her near a clock?"

Tim looked slightly dazed. I could see that he was already imagining himself in some swanky restaurant, drinking champagne with the rich and famous. It was time to bring him down to earth.

"You're not going," I said.

"Why not?" Tim replied.

"She's not interested in you, Tim. If she's invited you out, it's only for the publicity. That's all she cares about."

"Maybe she's got a soft spot for me."

"I don't think she's got a soft spot for anyone except herself. Anyway, she's a married woman."

"Listen, kid." Tim leant back in his chair. "You don't understand the female mind.

Maybe she's looking for something rough and a little bit dangerous."

"Then she can buy herself a yak."

"She likes me!"

"She's using you, Tim."

"She's invited me to dinner!"

"Well, if you're going, I'm going too."

Tim stared at me as if I'd just slapped him in the face – and I can't say I wasn't tempted. "Forget it, Nick," he said. "You heard what she said. This is a dinner for two. I don't need you there. I'm going on my own. And this time, my decision is final!"

The Gravy was one of London's most exclusive restaurants, reserved for celebrities and millionaires. It was so exclusive, even the waiters had trouble getting in, and the name was written in tiny letters as if it didn't want anyone to notice. It was tucked away in a quiet street near Covent Garden with a doorman sizing up everyone who came close. He looked at Tim and me with an expression of complete disgust. But this was the sort of place where even the doormat didn't say WELCOME. It preferred to say GO AWAY.

Why had I come? Part of the answer was that I was worried about Tim. I still didn't know what Minerva was up to, but I didn't trust her and I wanted to be there if things took a turn for the worse. But also, I quite fancied dinner at The Gravy. The food was said to be so good that the chef actually cried when you ate it. The house speciality was a leg of lamb cooked in Armagnac – and no matter that it cost you an Armagnac and a leg. Even a glass of water at The Gravy was expensive. It probably came out of a gold-plated tap.

The head waiter showed us to the best table, and there was Minerva looking stunning in a white silk dress that hugged her tight in all the right places and tighter still in some of the wrong ones. Her face fell when she saw me but she didn't protest as a couple of waiters hastily added a third setting to the table. It was only as we sat down that she muttered, "I'm surprised you brought your little brother, Timothy. Couldn't you find a babysitter?"

"I'm no baby, Minerva," I said.

"I was hoping to be alone with your big brother. I want to get to know him a little better."

"Just pretend I'm not here."

And that's exactly what she tried to do for the rest of the meal. The waiter came over with three menus but she chose only for the two of them, leaving me to decide for myself. That suited me. I went for the straightforward steak and chips, leaving the fancy stuff with the French names to her and Tim. If I've got one rule in life, it's never eat anything you can't translate.

"So tell me, Timothy," Minerva said, winking at him. "How would you like a little bubbly?"

Tim looked awkward. "Actually, I had a bath before I came."

"Bollinger!" she exclaimed.

"No. Really. I did!"

Minerva ordered a bottle of Bollinger. I asked for a Coke. The way she was making eyes at Tim, it really did seem that she had designs on him and I couldn't understand it. I mean, he was fifteen years younger than her and about fifty thousand times poorer. What could she see in him? I watched him as he opened the champagne for her. There was an explosive pop, followed by a scream from the other side of the room.

"The head waiter?" Tim asked.

"No," I said. "Just a waiter's head."

Minerva didn't seem to mind. She snuggled up close to him. "I love a man who makes me laugh," she said. "Can I ask you something, Timothy? Do you have a girlfriend?"

"Not at the moment," Tim answered.

"There's nobody waiting for you in bed tonight?"

"It's just Tim and his Paddington Bear hot-water bottle," I told her.

Tim glared at me.

"I fill it for him every night."

The waiter arrived with the first course:

soup for me, caviar for Tim and Minerva. Personally, I've never understood caviar. I mean, when I order eggs, I don't expect them to turn up tiny, black and fifty quid a mouthful. But she seemed happy enough. I wondered who would pick up the bill.

I could see that Tim was already well out of his depth. He was looking more and more uncomfortable the closer Minerva got, and she was already close enough. Any closer and she would be on his lap.

"Timothy ... I think you and I were meant for each other," she breathed.

"What about your husband?" Tim squeaked.

She sniffed. "Let's not talk about Harold. He's half the man you are."

"Which half are you talking about?"

I couldn't help chipping in again. "If you dislike him so much," I asked, "why did you marry him?"

To my surprise, Minerva looked me in the eye for the first time and I knew at once that she was going to be completely honest. "Why do you think?" she replied coldly. "I married Harold for his money. That was at the start of my career. I'd just left Athens and I had nothing. He promised to help me – and he did. Of course, all that's changed now. Now I'm worth millions!"

"So why are you still with him?"

"I can't be bothered to divorce him. Anyway, it's more fun the way things are."

"Does he know where you are tonight?"

Minerva laughed. "Of course he knows. You should have seen his face when I told him I was going out with Timothy. I thought he was going to have a heart attack!"

So that was why she had invited Tim to The Gravy. I should have seen it from the start. Minerva loathed her husband – that much had been obvious when we first met them at their suite at the hotel – and she amused herself by humiliating him. And what better way than to be seen out in public with someone like my big brother, Tim?

At that moment I disliked her as much as anyone I had ever known. More than Charon, the four-fingered assassin we met in Amsterdam. More than my homicidal French teacher, Monsieur Palis. The thing about Minerva was that she was beautiful, rich and loved by millions. But she had the heart of a snake.

Somehow we got through to the next course. My steak was fine but I didn't like the look of the grey, jelly-like dish that Minerva had ordered for herself and Tim. It came in a yellow sauce with rice and beans.

Tim wasn't sure either. He had eaten about half of it when he stopped and looked up. "What did you say this was?" he asked.

"*Cervelles de veaux au beurre.*"

He took another mouthful. "It tastes interesting," he said. "What does that mean?"

"Grilled calves' brains in butter."

Two minutes later we were standing outside on the pavement with the doorman glowering at us, glad to see us go.

"That was a nice evening," I said.

"Do you think Minerva enjoyed it?" Tim asked.

"Well, you may have spoiled it a bit when you were sick on her." I looked around for a bus or a taxi.

"I want to go home," Tim groaned. He was still looking very green.

"To Paddington Bear?"

"Just get us a cab!"

But as it turned out, we weren't going to need a bus or a cab. Because just then a car came screeching to a halt in front of us and two men leapt out.

"It's a police car!" Tim exclaimed.

That was particularly brilliant of him and I wasn't sure how he'd worked it out. Maybe it was the blue uniforms the men were wearing. Or it could have been the car with its flashing lights and the word POLICE emblazoned on the side. But he was right. I thought they'd come to look after Minerva – but it was the two of us they made for.

"Are you Tim Diamond?" one of them asked.

"Yes…"

"Get in the car. You're coming down to the station."

"What's going on?" I demanded. "What's happened? And how did you know we were here?"

They ignored me.

The policeman was examining Tim. "We want to talk to you," he said.

"What about?" Tim quavered.

The policeman smiled but without a shred of warmth or humour. It was the sort of smile a doctor might give you before he explained you only had a week to live. "You're wanted, Mr Diamond," he said. "For murder."

THE DEAD MAN

I don't like police stations. They're full of
violent and dangerous characters who need to
be kept away from modern society ... and I'm
not talking about the crooks. A lot of people
say the British police are wonderful, but I'd
have to disagree. I was only fourteen but I had
been arrested so often, it couldn't be long
before they gave me my own set of personal-
ized handcuffs. I even spent a month in prison
once – and I hadn't done anything wrong!
When I look back on it, there's only one word
to describe the way I've been treated. Criminal.

This time they drove us to a police station in
Holborn, about ten minutes' drive from The
Gravy. Tim had gone very pale and quiet in the
back of the car. *Cervelles de veaux au beurre*
and now this! We stopped and the two policemen led us in through a door and down the
usual corridor with white tiles on the walls and

hard neon lighting above … the sort of corridor that can only take you somewhere you don't want to be. There was an interrogation room at the end: four chairs, one table and two detectives. The furniture was hard and unattractive but that was nothing compared to the men.

Detective Chief Inspector Snape and Detective Superintendent Boyle. They were old friends and, like most of Tim's old friends, they hated us. Why was it that whenever we got into trouble, the two of them always seemed to show up? Surely the Metropolitan Police could have found two new officers to molest us? Anyway, put an ape and a Rottweiler in suits and you'll get a rough idea of Snape and Boyle. Snape was the older of the two and the one less likely to have rabies. He was looking old, I thought. But he'd probably looked old the day he was born.

"Well, this really is the perfect end to a horrible day," Snape began as we sat down. It didn't look as if he was going to offer us a cup of tea. "Tim Diamond! The only detective in London with no brains."

Tim went a little green.

"I wouldn't mention brains unless you know a good dry cleaner," I said.

"I want to go to bed!" Tim moaned.

"You're not going anywhere, Diamond," Snape cut in. "I'm investigating a murder and right now you're my only suspect."

"Can I hit him?" Boyle asked hopefully.

"No, Boyle."

"Can I hit his little brother?"

"No!"

"But they were resisting arrest, sir!"

"We haven't arrested them yet, Boyle." Snape shook his head and sighed. "I've just sent Boyle on an anger-management course," he told us.

"Did it work?" I asked.

"No. He got angry and hit the manager so they sent him back again."

"Well you're wasting your time," I said. "We haven't murdered anyone."

Snape looked at me with disdain. "What can you tell me about a man called Reginald Parker?" he said.

"I can't tell you anything, Snape," I said. "We've never met him."

"What's happened to him?" Tim asked.

"He's been murdered," Snape replied. "He was strangled this afternoon. He lived at 27 Sparrow Lane and his neighbour heard the sound of a fight. She called us and we found the body."

"What makes you think it's got anything to do with us?" I asked.

Snape nodded at Boyle. "Show them!"

Boyle leant down and produced a car battery connected to a tangle of wires with clamps on the end. He placed it on the table and glanced unpleasantly at Tim. Snape raised his eyes. "I don't mean that! I want you to show them the evidence!"

Boyle scowled. He opened a drawer and this time he produced a transparent evidence bag with something inside it. I recognized it at once. *No problem too problematic.* It was Tim's business card.

"We found this next to the body," Snape said. "How do you explain that?"

"A coincidence?" Tim suggested.

Snape's face darkened. "Of course it's not a coincidence, you idiot! It's a clue! Was Reginald Parker a client of yours? That wouldn't surprise me. Anyone stupid enough to hire you would almost certainly wind up dead."

I shook my head. "I told you, Chief Inspector. We've never seen him."

"How can you be so sure of that? I haven't even told you what he looked like."

Boyle opened the drawer a second time and produced a black and white photograph.

You can always tell when the police have taken a picture of someone after they're dead. They don't smile for the camera. In fact, they don't do anything. And the black and the white somehow seems to suit them. All the colour has already gone. The photograph showed a short, plump man with curly hair, lying on his back in the mess that had once been the room where he lived. I gasped. Because the truth was that I did know him. I had seen him once and only briefly, but it wasn't a face I was going to forget.

Reginald Parker was the man who had tried to shoot Minerva. He was the man on the roof above Regent Street.

"Did you find a gun in his room?" I asked.

Snape shook his head. "No. I told you. He was strangled."

"How about a handful of silver acorns? Or anything to do with oak trees?"

Boyle leant over the table and grabbed me by the collar. I felt myself being dragged to my feet. My feet left the floor. One of my shirt buttons went shooting over my shoulder. "Are you taking the mickey?" he demanded.

"No!" I gurgled. "I'm trying to help you. I did meet this man. I just didn't know his name."

Boyle turned to Snape, still holding me in the air. "Shall I wire him up to the car battery, sir?"

"Certainly not, Boyle!" Snape looked offended. "He's going to tell us everything anyway."

"I know that, sir. But this way he'll tell us quicker."

"Just put him down!"

Boyle looked on the edge of tears but he dropped me back into my seat. And then I told them everything that had happened since Jake Hammill had walked into our office. The meeting at the hotel. The events in Regent Street. Snape nodded when I talked about that. He must have seen Tim on the news.

"You're sure it was Parker on the roof?" he asked.

"It's the same face, Chief Inspector," I said.

"And you think he was a member of this organization – Overweight Albanian Kids?"

"He was certainly overweight." I nodded at the photograph.

"But as far as we know, he wasn't Albanian."

"Maybe he lived in Albania when he was young."

"We'll check it out."

"Does this mean you're letting us go?" Tim asked, getting to his feet.

"Not so fast, Diamond!"

"All right." Tim sat down, then got up more slowly.

Snape glowered. "I'll see you two again!" he said.

"Yeah. And I'll be waiting." Boyle was standing there holding one of the electrical contacts in his hand. The other was on the table. I passed it to him.

"Don't forget this," I said.

He took it in the other hand.

We could still hear Boyle screaming as we raced back down the corridor and out onto the street. But that's the modern police for you. Shocking.

When Tim and I had breakfast the next morning, I could see he was deep in thought. He didn't even react when he upturned the cereal packet and got the plastic toy.

"I just don't get it," he said at length.

"What's that, Tim?"

"Well ... this guy ... Archibald Porter."

"I think you mean Reginald Parker."

"He tried to kill Minerva and now somebody has killed him. But that doesn't make any sense. Nobody knew who he was. So why kill him? If they wanted to protect Minerva, they could have just reported him to the police."

He frowned but then his eyes brightened. "Maybe it was just another coincidence!" he exclaimed. "Maybe his death was an accident!"

"It's quite tricky to get strangled by accident," I pointed out.

Tim nodded. "I wonder how he got my business card?"

"That's exactly what we're going to find out..."

We were lucky that Snape had given us Parker's address. As soon as Tim had finished breakfast, we looked up Sparrow Lane in Tim's *A–Z*. Actually, it was an *A–W*. He'd got it cheap. Then we took a bus to the other side of London and a narrow street of terraced houses not far from the old meat market. Number 27 was halfway down and looked exactly the same as numbers 25 and 29 – apart, that is, from the policeman on duty and the blue and white POLICE LINE: DO NOT CROSS taped over the front door.

To be honest, I'd forgotten that Snape would have left someone on duty and I could see at a glance that we weren't going to get past the policeman at the door. He had the sort of face that if he ever decided to join the dog unit, he wouldn't need a dog. Ignoring him, I went straight to the house next door and rang the bell, hoping the owner would be in.

She was. The door opened and a huge, cheerful Caribbean woman in a brilliantly coloured dress appeared on the doorstep, the great slabs that were arms folded across her ample breast. "Yes, me darlings? How can I help you?" she boomed out.

I nudged Tim.

"I'm Tim Diamond," Tim said.

"Yes?" The woman was none the wiser.

"My brother is a private detective," I told her. "He wants to ask you some questions about the guy who lived next door."

"That's right," Tim explained. "And if he lived next door, then I'd imagine he must have been your neighbour."

"That's brilliant, Tim," I muttered. "How did you work that one out?"

It turned out that the woman was called Mrs Winterbotham and had lived at number 25 for almost as many years. Her husband was out, working at the meat market, and she invited us into her kitchen and gave us tea and coconut biscuits. She had already told the police everything but she was going to enjoy telling us again.

"Reginald was an actor," she said, then looked left and right and lowered her voice as if he might be listening from beyond the grave. "But he wasn't a very good one. Oh no! He was out of work most of the time. He was in *The Cherry Orchard* last May, playing one of the cherries. And last year he appeared at the Unicorn Theatre in a one-man show."

"Was it popular?" I asked.

"No. Only one man came." Mrs Winterbotham dropped three sugar cubes into her tea and helped herself to another biscuit. "Reginald was a nice man. But, you know, I'm not sure it really helped his career, his having a stutter."

I remembered now. Parker had stuttered when he was on the roof. So it hadn't been because he was afraid.

"I said to him that he ought to be a mime artist," Mrs Winterbotham went on. "That way he wouldn't have had to talk. But I don't think people would have paid to see him. He didn't have the figure for it. To be honest with you, I've seen more attractive figures hanging up in the meat market."

"When was his last job?" I asked.

"Well…" She put down the biscuit and leant forward conspiratorially. "That's what I told the police. He always got a job at Christmas. He worked in a department store. But this year something very unusual happened. He got paid for a one-night appearance in the West End! He didn't tell me what it was but I do know that it was a lot of money."

"Who paid him?"

"He never said. But I don't think it can have worked out because when I saw him the next morning, he was very upset."

"How do you know he was upset?" Tim asked.

"He was crying."

"You're sure they weren't tears of happiness?"

"Oh no, Mr Diamond. He was completely miserable. And then that afternoon, someone came to the house. I heard this banging and crashing and I went round to the garden to see what was happening. Then there was silence. I knocked on the door but I got no answer. So I called the police."

"Just one last question, Mrs Winterbotham…" I began.

"Please. Call me Janey!"

"Was Reginald Parker Albanian?"

"No. As far as I know, he'd never been to Albania. In fact, he never went anywhere. He couldn't afford it. Most of the time he just sat at home and watched TV." She sighed and I got the idea that maybe she'd been his only friend in the world. "And now he's dead. I can't believe it. Now, how about a nice piece of banana cake?"

We didn't have the cake.

Because suddenly, even as Mrs Winterbotham had been talking, everything had made sense. Suddenly I was back on the roof, hearing Reginald Parker as he called out across the gap. *I d-d-didn't...* I saw the cracker with the acorn and the death threat and knew what it was that was wrong with the letter Minerva had been sent. I thought about Regent Street and the bullet that had come so close it had drilled a hole in Harold Chase's coat. I knew exactly what job Reginald had been hired for – it could only be one job – and I also knew what was going to happen at twelve o'clock that day. I looked at my watch. It was five past eleven. We had less than one hour left.

"We have to get to Harrods, Tim!" I said.

Tim shook his head. "This is no time for Christmas shopping, Nick."

"We're not going shopping. We have to find Minerva."

"Why?"

A taxi drove by. I reached out and flagged it down.

"She's going to be murdered, Tim. And I know who by."

KILLER WITH A SMILE

We were on the wrong side of town. We had to cross the whole of London to reach Knightsbridge, and with Christmas just weeks away the traffic could hardly be worse. As we sat in a traffic jam on the edge of Hyde Park I could feel the minutes ticking away. Worse than that, I could see them. The taxi meter was running and Tim was staring at it in dismay, watching as the last of his earnings disappeared.

We finally made it with about five minutes and ten pounds to spare, but even so it was going to be tight. Harrods was a huge place and the grotto was right up on the fourth floor. Worse than that, the entire store was heaving – not just with shoppers but with the usual crowd of fans and policemen who had turned out to see or to protect Minerva. There were security men on all the doors and more photographers waiting in the street, although you'd have thought by now the papers would have had enough of her. I certainly had.

And what nobody knew was that the killer was already inside the building. He would smile at Minerva and he would murder her ... and she wouldn't even know it had happened until she woke up dead.

"This way, Tim!"

We had plunged off the street and into women's handbags, then into cosmetics, then food. Harrods was every Christmas present you could ever imagine – more presents than anyone in the world could ever want. It was Christmas gone mad: hundreds of miles of tinsel; thousands of glittering stars and balls; enough Christmas trees to repopulate a forest. Don't get me wrong. I love Christmas and I'll tear open as many presents as I can get my hands on. But as I ran for the escalators, past the groaning shelves and the grinning sales assistants, I couldn't help but feel there had to be something more to it than this. Maybe something less, if you know what I mean.

We reached the escalators and began to fight our way up. I had a strange sense of déjà vu as I went. Suddenly I was in another department store in a different part of London almost two years before. I'd been running then too – to escape from two German assassins who'd been trying to make sure that the only way I saw Boxing Day was from inside a box. But that was another time and another story and if you want to know about it, I'm afraid you're going to have to buy another book.

We got to the fourth floor and there was a sign pointing towards Santa's grotto, "Jingle Bells" blaring out of the speakers and little kids everywhere, dragging their mothers to see the man in red.

I stopped, panting. "I hope we're not too late," I gasped.

"Yes," Tim agreed. "Santa may not have any presents left!"

Sometimes I think Tim doesn't belong in the real world. Maybe he'd be more comfortable in a nice white room with padded walls. But this was no time to argue. It was twelve noon exactly. Somewhere in the clock department down below, a thousand clocks would be chiming, bleeping or shooting out cuckoos. The grotto had just been opened by Minerva. And the way ahead was blocked.

There were toys everywhere. Vast Lego castles, cuddly toys, jigsaw mountains and Scalextric cars buzzing round in furious circles. Children were pulling and pushing in every direction. In the far distance I could see the green, plastic entrance to a green, plastic cave with a long line of people waiting to go in. That was where we had to be. But our path had been closed off by a sixteen-stone store security guard with the body of a wrestler and the face of a boxer at the end of a particularly vicious fight. At least, I assumed he was a security guard. It was hard to be sure. He was dressed as an elf.

"You can't go this way!" he told me. "You have to go to the back of the queue." So he *was* a security guard. I should have known. How many elves do you see carrying truncheons?

"Where's Minerva?" I demanded. I was afraid I was already too late – and this brute in green tights was only making things worse.

"She's in with Santa Claus, opening the grotto. You'll have to wait in line if you want her autograph."

"I don't want her autograph. I want to save her life!"

But it was no good. I might as well have argued with Rudolph the Red-Nosed Reindeer (there was a mechanical version next to the cave). I had to stop myself pulling out my hair. I was expecting a gunshot at any moment and here I was trying to reason with an elf. I looked around me, wondering if I could bribe him with a cuddly toy – or if not, hit him with one. That was when I saw Detective Chief Inspector Snape, standing grim-faced with Boyle next to him, the two of them surrounded by Barbie dolls.

"Snape!" I shouted out, and before the

security guard could stop me I had run over to the two men.

"What are you doing here, Diamond?" he snapped the moment he saw me.

Boyle curled his lip and looked ugly – which in his case wasn't very difficult. Once again he lumbered forward and grabbed hold of me.

"Don't worry, Boyle!" I said. "I haven't come here to steal your Barbie doll."

"Then why are you here?" Snape demanded.

"You've got to find Minerva," I began. "She's in danger."

"I know she's in danger," Snape replied. "Boyle and I are on special duty. We're looking after her."

"You don't understand…"

How could I tell them what I knew? There wasn't enough time and with all the noise in the place – the children screaming, the music playing, Rudolph singing and all the rest of it – I'd have been hoarse before I got to the end. But just then Minerva appeared, coming out of the grotto with her manager, Jake Hammill, next to her. There was no sign of her husband, but somehow I wasn't surprised.

I twisted out of Boyle's grip, and with Tim right behind me I ran over to her. As usual, Minerva was looking drop-dead gorgeous in a slinky, silver number, and despite everything I was glad that I had arrived in time and that she hadn't, after all, dropped dead. She was holding a present, about the size and shape of a shoe box. Santa must have just given it to her.

She saw me. "You!" she snapped – and unless that's Greek for Happy Christmas, she wasn't too pleased to see me.

I stood in front of her, my eyes fixed on the box. I didn't want to touch it. To be honest, I didn't want to be anywhere near it. I had a good idea what was inside.

"Did Santa give you that?" I demanded.

"Yes." She nodded.

"Do you know what it is?"

Minerva shrugged. She didn't really care. She was only here for the publicity. "No," she said.

"I think it's a clock," Tim chimed in.

"Why?"

"Well … I can hear it ticking."

Snape leant forward and took the box. "What's all this about?" he demanded.

"Chief Inspector," I said, and suddenly my mouth was dry. "I'd be very careful with that unless you want to spend this Christmas in six different parts of London all at the same time."

"What are you talking about?" Hammill demanded.

"There's probably an oak leaf or two in there and maybe some acorns. But I'll bet you any money that the rest of it is a bomb."

Maybe I said the word too loudly. Somehow the crowd caught on to what was happening and suddenly the entire department was filled with hysterical mothers dragging their screaming kids off to the nearest escalator. I ignored them. I just wanted to know if Snape was going to believe me. And to be fair to him, just this once he gave me the benefit of the doubt. Very gently, he lowered the box to the ground, then turned to Boyle. "Have you got a knife?" he asked.

Boyle reached into his pocket and took out first a cut-throat razor, then a bayonet and finally a flick knife. He pressed a button and ten centimetres of ugly steel leapt out to join in the cheerful Christmas atmosphere. Snape took it. Very carefully, he cut a square in the side of the parcel and peeled the cardboard back. He looked inside.

"He's right!" he said.

He didn't need to tell me. Looking over his shoulder, I could just make out part of an alarm clock, some loops of wire and something that could have been Plasticine but definitely wasn't.

Snape looked up. "Plastic explosive," he whispered. "It's connected to an alarm clock. It'll blow up when the bell goes." He squinted through the square he had cut out. Then, very slowly, he handed the package to Boyle. "All right, Boyle," he said. "This is timed to go off in forty minutes. You'd better get it down to the bomb disposal squad."

"Where's that?" I asked.

"It's a forty-five-minute drive away."

Boyle stared at him.

"See if you can find a short cut," Snape advised.

Boyle disappeared – in a hurry. Snape turned to me. "So what's this all about?" he demanded.

"Santa just gave me that!" Minerva rasped. She was standing there dazed.

"Have you been a bad girl this year?" Tim asked.

"It's not Santa!" I said. "Come on…"

The five of us – me, Tim, Minerva, Jake Hammill and Snape – dived into the grotto. Out of the corner of my eye I saw the security guard talking into his radio, presumably calling for reinforcements. There was nobody else left on the fourth floor – as far as I knew, there was nobody left in Knightsbridge. White plastic snow crunched underfoot as we followed the path into the cave. White plastic stalactites hung down and white plastic stalagmites pointed up – or maybe it was the other way round. I can never remember. We passed a couple more mechanical singing reindeer and arrived just in time to see a familiar red figure, about to leave by a back exit.

"Hold it right there, Santa!" I shouted.

Santa froze, then slowly turned around.

"It's … it's … it's…!" Tim exclaimed. He stopped. He had no idea who it was, and with the red hood, the white beard and the golden-framed spectacles, I couldn't blame him. His own mother wouldn't recognize him. His own wife hadn't.

I walked forward and pulled off the beard. And there he was.

"Harold!" Minerva exclaimed.

"Harold?" Hammill quavered.

"That's right," I said. "Harold Chase."

There could be no doubt about it. The old man reached up and lowered the hood, revealing more of his face, his silver hair and his hearing aid. He had concealed his permanent suntan with make-up. But there could be no disguising the venom with which he was looking at his wife.

Snape took over. "You just gave Minerva a bomb," he said.

Harold Chase said nothing.

"That's a very original present," Tim commented.

"Not really, Tim," I said. "He was trying to kill her."

It was the word "kill" that did it. The bomb had been taken away. But Harold Chase exploded. "I hate her!" he screamed. "You have no idea what it's been like living with her! I know why she married me. She wanted my money! But now that she's so big and so famous she doesn't need me. And so she humiliates and belittles me. She's made my life hell!"

He took a step towards us. Tim took three steps back.

"But that's not the worst of it," Harold went on. "She's a hypocrite. She smiles at the crowds on Regent Street when secretly she despises them. She hates Christmas too – and every year she's ruined it for me. No carols, no presents, no tinsel, no fun. She's stolen Christmas from me and that was a good enough reason to want to see her dead."

By now, he was frothing at the mouth and I almost wished Boyle was there to deal with him. Fortunately the security guard disguised as an elf had appeared with two colleagues, and the three of them dragged Harold out. He was still screaming as he went.

The five of us went back downstairs to a champagne bar on the ground floor. It was somewhere quiet and we had a lot to talk about. Minerva paid for champagne for herself and the others. I got a glass of lemonade. I had to admit she seemed very shaken by what had happened. Her face was pale. Her eyes were thoughtful. And even her silver-plated breasts seemed to have lost their sparkle.

"All right, Diamond," Snape said, emptying his glass. "Spit it out!"

"He hasn't drunk anything yet," Tim said.

"I want you to tell me what's been going on. How did you know about Harold Chase and how did you figure out his plan?"

"I worked it out when we visited Janey Winterbotham," I explained.

"The next-door neighbour?" Snape sniffed. "I spoke to her. She didn't tell me anything."

"She told me that Reginald Parker was an out-of-work actor but that he had a job in a department store every Christmas," I said. "What else could he have been but a department store Santa? That was when it all fell into place."

"Why don't you start at the beginning?" Jake Hammill suggested.

"All right." I drew a breath. "This is the way I see it. Harold Chase hated Minerva for all the reasons he just told us. His hatred had obviously driven him mad and he decided to kill her. But the trouble was, it was too obvious. If Minerva died, he would be the main suspect. Everyone knew how badly she treated him."

"A lot of people would die to be married to me," Minerva sniffed.

"He *was* married to you – and you were the one he wanted to die," I reminded her. "Anyway, Harold couldn't kill you himself. He'd be arrested at once. But then he had an idea. He realized that the best way to get rid of you was to create someone who didn't exist:

81

a crazy fan. He used that concert you cancelled – for Overweight Albanian Kids – and pretended that someone was out to get revenge."

"You mean ... it was Harold who wrote that anonymous letter?" Hammill asked.

"Exactly. He even put a fake spelling mistake in it – but if he couldn't spell 'forgive', how come he could spell 'forget' a few lines later? The whole thing felt fake to me."

"And what about the cracker?"

"That was another clue. I thought at the time that there was something weird about it, but it was only later that I realized what it was." I turned to Hammill. "You'd booked Minerva into the Porchester hotel under a false name."

"Right," he said.

"But the box of crackers was addressed to her. Whoever sent it even knew the number of the suite where she was staying. It had to be an inside job."

"But wait a minute," Snape interrupted. "If it was Chase all the time, what was Reginald Parker doing on the roof at Regent Street?"

"Reginald Parker had been paid by Chase," I explained. "His neighbour told us he got a lot of money for a job in the West End. She probably thought it was a job in theatre. My guess is that Chase paid him to leave the silver oak leaves on the roof. Parker had no idea what he was doing. He didn't have a gun or anything. I saw him carrying something, but it could have been a camera. After all, he knew Minerva was there. He was a complete innocent. That's what he tried to tell me when I went up there. 'I didn't...' That was all he managed. But what he wanted to say was, 'I didn't do it!' He must have been horrified when he heard the shots."

"So who *did* shoot at me?" Minerva asked. She poured herself some more champagne. I wondered what she was celebrating. Maybe it was the fact she was still alive.

"That was Harold," I said. "Again, I'm only guessing, but I'd say he fired two blank shots from a gun he had inside his pocket. When we were on the platform, the shots sounded very close. He fired twice and then pointed to Reginald up on the roof – because, of course, he knew he'd be there. You see, he was creating the illusion of a killer ... someone who didn't really exist. The only snag is, the gun burnt a hole in his coat." I glanced at Minerva. "You thought he'd almost been hit. In fact, he'd fired the shots himself."

"I don't get it," Minerva exclaimed. "He wanted to protect me! It was Harold who persuaded me to get a bodyguard!"

"He did that to throw off any suspicion. At the same time, he made sure you hired the worst private detective in London. Someone too stupid to get in the way of his plan."

"And who was that?" Tim asked.

"Have some more champagne, Tim," I said.

"And then Harold Chase killed Reginald Parker," Snape said.

"You've got it in one, Chief Inspector. Chase had chosen Parker because he knew he was going to be the Santa Claus at Harrods. First of all he hired him to go on the roof. Then he killed him and took his place. Tim's business card must have fallen out of his pocket during the fight. It was when I saw the card that I put two and two together..."

"You did your maths homework?" Tim asked.

"No, Tim. I cracked the case."

There was a long silence. Either I'd been talking too slowly or they'd been drinking too quickly but all the champagne was gone. And I hadn't even touched my lemonade.

Jake Hammill put an arm around Minerva. "Baby, I'm so sorry," he said. "What a terrible experience for you!"

Minerva shrugged. "It wasn't so bad," she said. "I've got rid of Harold. I'm going to get lots of publicity. And my CD's certain to go to number one." She got to her feet. I thought she was going to leave, but she took one last look at me. "You're quite smart for a scruffy fourteen-year-old," she said. Then she flicked her eyes towards Tim. "As for you, you're just an utter loss."

She walked out.

"What did she mean?" Tim wailed.

I thought for a moment. "Justanutterloss. It's Greek for sensational," I said.

"Really?" Tim's eyes lit up.

"Sure, Tim," I said. Well, after all, it was Christmas.

There are a few things to add.

Two weeks later, Tim and I got a surprise in the post – and this time it wasn't a bomb, an unpaid bill or a poison pen letter. It was a note from Jake Hammill. It seemed that he wasn't so bad after all. We had just saved his most famous client from a murder attempt that would have been not only the end of her career, but – even worse – the end of his percentage. And as a token of his gratitude, he'd decided to send us a cheque for ten thousand pounds. I'll never forget the sight of Tim holding it between his hands. The last time he had seen that many zeros, it had been in his school report.

We talked a lot about what to do with the money. Of course, we were going to have a proper Christmas lunch. Tim was going to pay off the rent. I was finally going to get a new school uniform – the last one had so many patches in it, it was more patches than uniform. But that would still leave us with several thousand pounds, which was just about the most money we'd ever had.

I forget who suggested it first, but that was when we decided to fly out to Australia to be reunited with our parents. It had been years since we'd seen them, and sometimes I thought it was unnatural for a young lad to be living without his mother, often crying himself to sleep, having to be tucked in every night and cheered up by his brother. Not that I minded doing all that for Tim, but even so I thought it would do us all good to be a family again, just for a while.

And the next day we bought two British Airways tickets to Sydney. We were going to travel out as soon as the Easter term ended, and maybe one day I'll write down what actually happened when we got there. *The Radius of the Lost Shark*. That's the title I've got written down in my notebook. It's another story I've got to tell.

What else is there? Harold Chase got life in jail for attempted murder, but looking at him I didn't think that would be too many years. Snape took the credit for the arrest, of course. They actually put his face on the front cover of the monthly police journal, *Hello, Hello, Hello* magazine. Reginald Parker's remains were scattered in the River Thames, in front of the National Theatre – as he'd requested in his will. It can't have been pleasant, though. He hadn't been cremated.

And what about Minerva? She may have got to number one, but I didn't care. I never listened to her music again. She may have had everything, but without a heart you're just nothing. She was like a December without Christmas – and at the end of the day, what's the point of that?

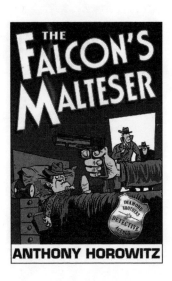

*Johnny Naples opened his mouth and
tried to speak. "The falcon..." he said.
Then a nasty, bubbling sound...*

When vertically challenged Johnny Naples entrusts
Tim Diamond with a package worth over three
million pounds, he's making a big mistake. For Tim
Diamond is probably the worst detective in the
entire world.

Next day, Johnny's dead. Tim gets the blame,
his smart, wisecracking younger brother Nick gets
the package – and every crook in town is out to get
them!

PUBLIC ENEMY
NUMBER TWO

DIAMOND
BROTHERS

DETECTIVE
AGE

ANTHONY HOROWITZ

So there I was in a maximum-security prison
outside London, accused of theft, trespass,
criminal damage and cruelty to animals…
Me, public enemy number two!

Framed for jewel robbery, quick-thinking young
Nick Diamond finds himself sharing a prison
cell with Johnny Powers, Public Enemy Number
One. His only chance of rescuing the situation is to
nail the Fence, the country's master criminal.

But first, Nick has to get out of jail – which is
where his older brother Tim, the world's worst
private detective, comes in. And with Ma Powers and
her gang waiting to greet the jailbirds, the heat is
really on!

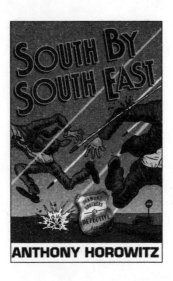

*McGuffin had finished talking. The telephone
was dead and any minute now he'd be joining it.
The stuff he had spilled down his coat was
blood, his own blood...*

Tim Diamond, the world's most defective private
detective, is broke – as his much smarter younger
brother Nick is quick to remind him. So when a mysterious stranger offers Tim a wad of money for his
overcoat, it seems like a stroke of good luck.

But there are worse things in life than being broke.
Being pumped full of lead, for one – which is what
happens to the stranger and could soon be the fate of
the Diamond brothers unless they can outwit the
unknown assassin on their tail!

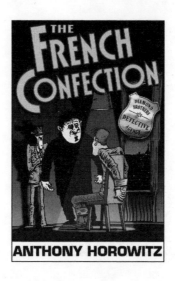

"Tim," I asked. "What's the French for murder?"
Tim shrugged. "Why do you want to know?"
"I've got a feeling it's something we're
going to need..."

When the hard-up Diamond brothers win a weekend
for two in Paris, it looks like their luck is taking a turn
for the better. But looks can be deceptive.

No sooner have they arrived in the French capital
than the brothers are up to their necks in danger.
There's a nasty smell in the air and it's not the cheese.
If Nick and Tim aren't careful, their dream holiday
could end up being a nightmare from which they'll
never wake...

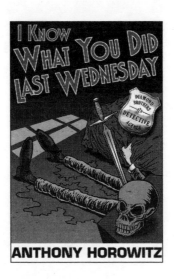

It's not fair. I do my homework.
I clean my teeth twice a day.
Why does everyone want to kill me?

It's a dangerous life being the younger brother of the world's worst private detective – but Nick Diamond has survived ... so far. He's due a holiday, so he should be happy when his brother Tim receives an invitation to a school reunion on a remote Scottish island.

But Nick's got a bad feeling, and it's not indigestion. When he meets their fellow guests, the feeling only gets worse. Especially when they start dying in ever more bizarre ways... Could it be the Diamond brothers' days are numbered?

ANTHONY HOROWITZ

"My name is Carter," he said at last.
He spoke with an American accent.
"Joe Carter. I've just got in from Chicago.
And I've got a problem."

The man in the photo is so blurry, it's impossible to make out what he really looks like. And that's before he was run over by a steamroller! His name was Lenny Smile and he ran a children's charity called Dream Time, financed by millionaire author Joe Carter.

Now Carter wants to know just what happened to Smile – and to the money. Unfortunately he's hired Tim Diamond, the world's most defective private detective, to find out!

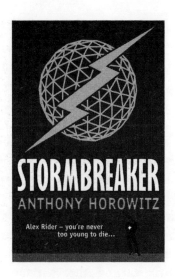

Meet Alex Rider, the world's most reluctant spy.

Forcibly recruited into MI6 after the mysterious death of his guardian, fourteen-year-old Alex is sent to infiltrate the organization of a sinister billionaire. Within days he's gone from schoolboy to superspy – and it looks like his first assignment may be his last...

"Every bored schoolboy's fantasy, only a thousand times funnier, slicker and more exciting ... genius."
The Independent on Sunday

Now a major motion picture starring Alex Pettyfer!

ANTHONY HOROWITZ is one of the most popular and prolific children's writers working today. His phenomenally successful Alex Rider series, comprising *Stormbreaker*, *Point Blanc*, *Skeleton Key*, *Eagle Strike*, *Scorpia*, *Ark Angel* and *Snakehead*, has sold over ten million copies worldwide and won numerous awards, including the Booksellers Association/Nielson Author of the Year Award 2007, the Children's Book of the Year Award for *Ark Angel* at the 2006 British Book Awards and the Red House Children's Book Award for *Skeleton Key* in 2003. *Stormbreaker*, the first Alex Rider mission, was recently made into a blockbuster movie starring Alex Pettyfer as the teenage superspy.

Anthony's other titles for Walker Books include the hugely popular Diamond Brothers mysteries; *Groosham Grange* and its sequel, *Return to Groosham Grange*; *The Devil and His Boy*; *The Switch*; *Granny*; and The Power of Five, a series of supernatural thrillers beginning with *Raven's Gate*, *Evil Star* and *Nightrise*.

Anthony also writes extensively for TV, with credits including *Midsomer Murders*, *Poirot* and the drama series *Foyle's War*, which won the Lew Grade Audience Award in 2003. He is married to television producer Jill Green and lives in London with his two sons, Nicholas and Cassian, and their dog, Unlucky. You can find out more about Anthony and his books by visiting his website, at:

www.anthonyhorowitz.com